THE COMPASS AND THE SINGING RIVER

ANWITA KEDILAYA

Foreword

Step into the quiet corners of BEURIO, a city where secrets sleep beneath. In this world, we meet Anika, a young girl whose imagination fills the silence of her days. But imagination is only the beginning. When a mysterious book with golden writing and a silver key finds its way into her hands. So, prepare to follow her into the echoing chambers of the past.

Acknowledgements

I have taken a lot of effort in this book however it would not have been possible without the help and support of many individuals.

Firstly, I would thank The Sanskaar Valley School for providing this beautiful opportunity to me. It would not have been possible without the help of my kind mentors at the school.

A big thanks to my Parents for believing in me and helping me throughout the entire journey. You are my strength and my greatest gift from God.

I will be failing in my efforts if i do not thank my creativity partner my brother Yuvaan, for all his creative ideas.

Above all I thank the Almighty for putting in thoughts in my enthusiastic mind at the right time.

CHAPTER ONE

THE BOOK IN THE STACKS

In the beautiful city of BEURIO lived a little 11year old girl named Anika. She had lost her father at a very young age and her mother could barely make ends meet, working multiple jobs just to keep a roof over their heads.

Little Anika trudge back from school each day to an empty house, her small backpack slung over her shoulder and her shoes dusty from the long walk home. The walls of the empty house echoed with silence, Anika always filled it with her laughter and imagination. But imagination was not the only thing that kept her going—it was her deep curiosity and love for story books.

Every evening, she would visit the tiny library at the end of the street. The librarian was an elderly man named Mr. Otto, who had known Anika's father.

The library smelled of old paper and lavender. And the books seemed to whisper secrets when no one was looking. One day when Anika was in the library, she came across a section of books she had not seen before. She picked up a book with golden writing on the spine.   Its pages were filled with elegant, swirling handwriting—almost too perfect to be human. The first line read:

"To the one who finds the key, beware: not all doors lead forward."

Her fingers shook slightly as she touched the silver key. Which was embedded in the thick pages of the book.

That night, Anika slipped the key under her pillow, and her dreams were strange.

The next morning, Anika couldn't shake the strange feeling the book and that key had given her. She tucked the silver key into her coat pocket, along with the mysterious book, and set off for school. But she didn't go straight there.

Instead, she took a detour through the oldest part of Beurio, where the buildings leaned over the narrow-cobbled streets.

That part of the city was forgotten and faded from everybody's memories.

But something caught Anika's eye: a strange mulberry bush. When she went up to it for closer inspection, she found that there was a door behind it. And to her surprise the key fit perfectly into it.

Anika thought to herself was this the end of the mystery, but greater did she know she had been kept away from a huge family secret.

CHAPTER TWO

THE DOOR BENETH THE CITY

The door creaked open—not into a room, but into darkness. Cold air rushed out, smelling like something old, like forgotten earth.

She leaned forward, peering in.

On the other side was a stone staircase leading down… but the strangest part was the air inside the doorway—it shimmered, like a heatwave, even though the day was cool.

The stone steps spiralled downward. Anika's footsteps echoed in the silence, but she wasn't afraid not yet. She clutched the book tightly to her chest and kept going,

After what felt like forever, she reached the bottom.

She found herself in a corridor; walls of which were filled with paintings of people. It looked like they all belonged to the same big, happy family. At the end of the corridor was an arch way. When Anika walked through it, she entered a room which had a pedestal in the centre, and on it was a small stone box. As her fingers touched the lid, the symbols on the walls began to glow.

She opened the box.

Inside was a folded piece of parchment and a single black feather. It read:

"To find the map, seek the place where time forgets, and water remembers."

Before she could read it again, a low hum filled the chamber, and the stone box sealed itself shut. A faint breeze stirred the feather. It lifted, hovered in the air for a moment then drifted toward a hidden crack in the wall.

Anika didn't hesitate and followed the feather into a tunnel that curved upward.

The tunnel led her to an overgrown garden behind an abandoned greenhouse. Anika sat on a cracked stone bench nearby. And tried to solve the riddle but it was of no use.

Her gaze then drifted to the greenhouse.

It had once been a part of the beautiful city, but the place was now forgotten.

In the centre stood a large, dry fountain. She walked over, brushing vines aside, and saw a strange symbol etched into the bottom of the fountain bowl. She had seen the same symbol earlier in the tunnel.

She knelt beside it. Something glinted. A coin?

No—*a **compass.*** But it didn't have any needles. Anika sensed something strange about this. So, she decided to go back to the library to ask Mr. Otto.

But one thing she had understood that this wasn't just a treasure hunt. This was a test!

And someone or something was leaving her clues for a reason.

CHAPTER THREE

THE COMPASS WITHOUT NEEDLES

After about a five-minute walk Anika reached the library. The familiar scent of lavender and old parchment calmed her racing heart. Mr. Otto looked up from the front desk, his eyes widening slightly when he saw what she carried.

With a smile on his face, he said "So you found it."

Anika was confused but nodded slowly and said "In the old greenhouse. Behind the fountain."

Well, you're further along than I thought, he said "Much further."

Mr. Otto closed his eyes for a moment, then reached beneath the desk and pulled out a dusty wooden box. It said:

"Property of Arthur"

Arthur was Anika's father. "This," he said, placing it before her, "was written by your father. I was told to give it to you only when the compass returned to the library in your hands."

Anika was absolute flabbergast on hearing this. She was angry with Mr. Otto for not telling her sooner but at the same time she felt a sense of relief. And so, when she opened the box inside were the needles to the compass and a letter.

"My dear Anika, If you're reading this, then the path has found you. This journey isn't about treasure. It's about our family and our hidden legacy not just in time, but in memory. You'll need courage, wit, and above all, kindness. The compass will guide you, but only when your heart is steady. The place where time forgets and water remembers... that's where the truth begins."
Love,
Papa

Anika was upset after reading this but not as much as she was determined to find the truth. She understood the urgency of the words he had left for her.

Mr. Otto watched her closely and said "The map you seek isn't drawn in ink. It's drawn in memory. Places touched by your family, stories passed down—forgotten by most, but not by the water."

Anika knew she had to uncover this mystery and find the hidden legacy.

"The compass will show you the path only when you understand the places it leads you to" said Mr. otto.

CHAPTER FOUR

OFF TO THE MONASTRY

After fixing the needles on the compass. Anika left the library, the cool breeze of BEURIO greeted her, but it felt different now. The air had changed with purpose.

The compass in her hand spun aimlessly. And did not point towards a direction.

Each beat led her thoughts back to the letter:

"The place where time forgets, and water remembers..."

Soon she came across a place where monks once kept sacred records not on paper but carved into stone and sung into wells. It had been abandoned for decades; it was a Monastery. People believed it held memories.

Inside, it was very quiet, not a soul to be heard.

Anika stumbled upon some rocks that protruded out of the surface and as Anika stepped forward, the compass reacted again it began spinning aimlessly.

A figure emerged, out from the shadows cast by the falling stone. It was an old woman dressed in deep blue robes that glistened in the moonlight like water. Despite her old age, her eyes had an odd clarity.

"You carry Aurther's compass" she said in a low voice.

Anika tightened her grip on the compass as she froze. "You knew my father?" she said.

"Arthur came here, long ago. Just as lost, as determined and left more than secrets behind." The woman replied.

Anika now confused asked the woman who she was, to which the woman replied "I am the Keeper of this Monastery"

CHAPTER FIVE

ECHOES IN THE WATERS

Anika followed the Keeper as they walked through winding halls lit only by moonlight streaming through broken stained glass.

They reached an underground chamber—its walls covered in the same symbols she had seen before in the tunnel and a large circular well at its centre. The Keeper signalled for Anika to come closer. "This well remembers voices"

Anika knelt and peered in. The compass in her hand began to glow and then she heard a sweet familiar voice.

IT WAS HER MOTHER'S VOICE

But there were two voices, singing in harmony. The voice sounded like her own voice.

Who is that she asked the keeper. The Keeper closed her eyes.

"The water remembers that day your mother showed up with two daughters, and One was taken to protect the other." Anika gaped, unbelieving. "Two daughters? You mean..." "Yes dear," said the keeper. But who was the second daughter. Said Anika, still confused.

To which the keeper replied, "Your twin my dear."

CHAPTER SIX

THE OATH OF SILENCE

Anika's head was spinning. A twin? "Why... why was she taken? Where is she now?" Anika's voice was now trembling.

The keeper reached into a pocket of her robe and brought out a little dusty bottle, full of a shimmering liquid.

"This liquid contains memory. But those who take the Oath are the only ones who will hear the truth that is held."

What is the oath asked Anika. **The Oath Of Silence** said the keeper.

Once drunk you will see what others cannot and what has been hidden for too long!

Anika plucked up the courage if not for her, for her sister. "I am ready to drink it she said"

Before gulping the entire bottle. "Repeat after me," said the keeper.

"By silence I hear. By memory I see. Let what was hidden; now flow through me."

Everything went dark and they were not in the Monastery anymore.

They stood in a memory.

It was raining. Anika watched a younger version of her mother—a woman with tired eyes and trembling hands walking up to the well.

In her arms, she held two baby girls, wrapped in matching cloth. There at a distant stood young Arthur.

CHAPTER SEVEN

RIVER LYRA

"They'll come for them," her mother whispered almost too scared to speak properly. "The prophecy is too dangerous."

Arthur placed a hand on her shoulder. "Then we shall split the key." He spoke

"One child will carry the compass. The other will carry the map" They kissed the foreheads of both babies. Then, a robed figure of the Keeper stepped from the shadows.

"I will take one to the river's cradle. She'll be safe there." she said

Her mother cried but nodded. One baby was handed over and the other stayed.

The vision blurred and faded.

Anika collapsed to her knees. She had just watched the moment were she and her sister were torn apart.

The Keeper's voice was soft beside her. "Your sister's name is **Manika.** She still lives but the map inside her can only be seen when you're together.

Anika wiped her eyes. "Where is she?"

Where the river sings. Where the compass first spins true."

And with that, the compass in Anika's hand started to hum again—and for the first time was pointing due east.

which river? she asked the keeper

The Keeper's gaze softened. "There is a river that winds through the eastern edge of BEURIO" Named Lyra.

The journey was far from over. But for the first time since finding the mysterious book, Anika felt a surge of hope. Her sister was out there, somewhere along the singing river, and Anika would find her.

CHAPTER EIGHT

IN THE SINGING WATER

Following the subtle guidance of the compass, Anika continued her journey along the river Lyra.

The river eventually led her to a more secluded part of the valley, where the water widened. The air hummed with the sound of unseen insects.

Suddenly her eye caught a tiny cottage.

Hesitantly, she knocked on the cottage door. It creaked open to reveal a young woman with eyes that mirrored her own.

A gasp escaped Anika's lips.

"Manika?"

The young woman's eyes widened in surprise, then filled with a dawning recognition.

"Anika?" she replied. Tears welled in both their eyes as they rushed towards each other, embracing in a long, overdue hug.

But their joyous reunion was short-lived. As the sisters sat by the window, sharing their stories a shadow fell across the doorway. It was a mighty figure, **Andras**.

"So," the Andras gasped, "The two halves of the key have finally come together."

Anika quickly moved closer to Manika, a sense of dread washing over her. This was not a friendly visitor.

"Who are you?" she demanded. Andras chuckled. "Someone who understands the true power of your family's legacy." He took a step closer, his eyes fixed on Manika. "The map within you will soon be mine, child."

Manika clutched Anika's hand; her eyes wide with fear. Certainly, their union had not gone unnoticed. The true test of their journey had just begun.

CHAPTER NINE

THE WOLF AT THE RIVER'S EDGE

The sight of Manika' s terrified face ignited a spark of defiance within Anika. She stepped in front of Manika.

"Stay away from her," Anika warned, her voice stronger than she felt.

"Foolish girl. You have no idea what power you possess together. Power that has been hidden for generations, a power I intend to claim." Replied Andras.

Manika instinctively touched her chest, a sudden understanding dawning in her eyes.

"You won't get it," Manika declared, finding strength in her sister's presence.

Suddenly, the compass in Anika's pocket began to spin wildly. "The artifacts react to your presence," the figure hissed, taking another step closer. "They recognize a threat to their purpose."

Anika knew they couldn't fight him here. The cottage offered no escape. Her eyes darted around the room, desperately searching for a way out. The back window.

"Manika, run!" Anika shouted, shoving her sister towards the back of the cottage.

Before Manika could react, the cloaked figure lunged forward.

Manika, startled but spurred by Anika's command, scrambled towards the back window. It was jammed.

Andras turned his attention to Manika, "Trying to escape, little map?" Anika seized the opportunity. She grabbed a heavy wooden stool and swung it at the figure's back

With a final desperate heave, the window sprang open.

"Anika, come on!" Manika cried

"You cannot escape me!" the cloaked Andras roared.

The sisters didn't wait. They fled into the dense woods.

CHAPTER TEN

THE SPINE OF FEAR

They ran until their lungs burned and their legs ached. They huddled together, their hearts pounding listening to the heavy breathing and frustrated growls of their pursuer as he searched for them in the fading light.

Trapped and hunted, the sisters knew their reunion had come at a dangerous price.

The mystery of their family's legacy was far more perilous.

"He wants the map inside you," Anika whispered, her hand gripping Manika's tightly. "What does he mean?

Manika shook her head, her brow furrowed in concentration. "I don't know exactly. But ever since we were separated, I've had… feelings…. Images…. Fleeting glimpses of places and symbols…

It's like a story waiting to be told, but I could never quite grasp it symbols… It's like a story waiting to be told, but I could never quite grasp it."

"The compass is useless like this," Anika said, frustration lacing her voice. "It usually guides, but now it just reflects our panic."

Suddenly, Manika gasped. "Wait! When he mentioned the artifacts reacting... maybe that's the key. They aren't meant to work in fear. They need... harmony."

"We need to calm down," Anika realized. "Both of us. Maybe then the compass will settle." Taking deep breaths, the sisters focused on each other

Manika closed her eyes:

I'm seeing... a pattern," she murmured, her voice barely above a whisper. "Swirling lines... like water... and symbols... the same ones from the monastery and the fountain... but they're moving, connecting..."

"River Lyra is not just a place; it's part of the map!" she shrieked.

They moved stealthily, aware that Andras could still be nearby. The map wasn't just within Manika; it was a connection to the land itself, a memory etched into the water and the stones.

CHAPTER ELEVEN

SHADOWS 'S PURSUIT

As they journeyed upstream, Manika's visions grew stronger. Each place resonated with the "map" within her, unlocking fragments of their family's history.

They learned that their ancestors were guardians of a powerful knowledge.

The cloaked figure, however, was not far behind. He seemed to possess an uncanny ability to track them.

When Manika touched a flat, smooth stone by the river, a clear memory came to her, and she told Anika about it.

They saw their parents standing there, younger and full of hope, their father carefully explaining the river's significance and the connections between their family's legacy. "

The prophecy..." Anika murmured, remembering her mother's whispered words in the vision. "He knows about it. And I think... I think our ancestors knew someone would come for this knowledge."

Their journey led them to an ancient grove, where the Lyra flowed into a small creek.

As they reached the water's edge, Andras emerged from the shadows, blocking their path.

His hood had fallen back during his relentless pursuit, revealing a huge face. His cold eyes held obsession.

Anika and Manika stood together, no longer just lost sisters, but united guardians of their family's legacy, sensing that the final test was in front, and perhaps a hidden inheritance, awaited them at this sacred place.

CHAPTER TWELVE

BEGINING OF THE END

"The map isn't something you can take," Manika declared, her voice surprisingly steady. "It's part of us, part of this place."

Andras tried to attack them….

Anika and Manika moved as one. But suddenly Anika remembered the silver key in the book and reached into her pocket and grasped it tightly.

As the cloaked figure attacked again, Anika held out the silver key.

It resonated with the energy from the stone and the pool, emitting a faint, silvery hum. The compass in her hand, now perfectly still, pointed directly at the key.

The tall Andras staggered back, clutching his head. "What is this? Lies! Illusions!" he cried,

They could see their ancestors in front on then as though protecting them from the gaint Andras.

"It's not illusions," Anika said, her voice filled with dawning understanding. "It's the truth of what happened here.

Andras, weakened and disoriented by the visions, stared at the alcove with a mixture of rage and despair.

The cloaked figure weakened and disoriented. Before he could react, another surge of energy from the pool washed over him, finally bringing an end to him.

The sisters happy after the win then proceeded to find the treasure, Their family's true hidden legacy.

The map led them back to the singing river. This location was clearly significant as it was deliberately hidden by their ancestors.

As they spoke the ground nearby started to shift; it was like an earthquake. Manika grabbed Anika's hand in fear.

As the dust settled slightly, they could see that the crack widened into a narrow opening, into darkness. The shift in the ground almost as if triggered by their presence. They knew they had to find out more, so they decided to descend into the darkness.

At the end of the staircase, they saw huge corridor there in the corner was a broken, old lantern which they lit using stones. "Look at these carvings". There were carvings depicting scenes of their ancestors. In one part of the wall, the carvings showed their ancestors hiding something, their faces determined.

By now they knew this wasn't just a hidden passage; It was a step towards finding their family legacy.

CHAPTER THIRTEEN

RETURN TO BEURIO

Manika, holding the lantern steady, followed her gaze. "It's like a history book etched in stone. And the symbols… they're more detailed here, almost telling a story."

"This place… it feels alive," she murmured, a sense of connection washing over her. "Like the earth itself is breathing.

The corridor seemed to go on forever. But when they finally reached the end, they saw a huge 15 Feet stone wall. In the middle was a triangled shaped hole in the wall.

It matched a stone fallen on the ground. Manika picked it up and tried to fit it into the hole. And to their surprise it fit perfectly.

The gateway opened into a big room. The ceiling was so high up that they could barely see it.

The entire room was filled with valuable paper, scripts and scrolls, evidence of early medical practices in India, archaeological discoveries from various periods and religions providing insights into legal cultural and philosophical systems of time to understand our cultural roots and evolution of human civilization.

    Anika and Manika were thrilled to witness this. They finally found their legacy, for what their family had sacrificed so much so that this ancient knowledge could be preserved. It was protected from the evil tribes from where the people like Andras came. These preaching could have been misused for destruction of the mankind in the quest to become the supreme power by the evil.

Standing together Anika and Manika looked at each other with tears in their eyes.

They had not only found each other and stopped a threat, but they had also inherited profound responsibility.

Finally, they returned to BEURIO, not as lonely individuals, but as sisters with immense responsibility of protecting their family treasure for the generations to come....

Keywords

SILVER KEY

MAP

MONASTARY

LIBRARY

HIDDEN TREASURE

COMPASS